D0368867

Tales of

Brer Rabbit

Tales of
Brer Rabbit

Retold by Stephanie Laslett

|| • PARRAGON • ||

A PARRAGON BOOK

Published by
Parragon Publishing,
Queen Street House, 4 Queen Street,
Bath BA1 1HE

Produced by
The Templar Company plc,
Pippbrook Mill, London Road, Dorking,
Surrey RH4 1JE

Printed and bound in China.
ISBN 0 75253 146 8

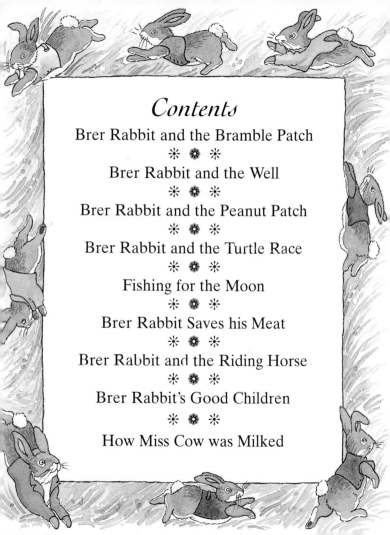

Contents

HISTORY

The *Brer Rabbit* stories began as American Negro fables, told by the slaves working on plantations in the deep South of North America, and almost certainly African in origin.

Joe Chandler Harris (1848-1908) insisted that he did no more than simply retell the stories, but in fact he showed great storytelling skill in padding out what was often little more than a folk saying. He also retained the wonderfully rich dialect of the southern Negro slaves, writing the words just as they would have been said. This text has been adapted for easier reading and understanding, but still retains the flavour of Uncle Remus's relaxed storytelling style.

Many years ago on a cotton plantation down in the deep south of North America there lived an old black slave called Uncle Remus. Every evening as the sun set behind the persimmon trees and the shadows lengthened across the dusty yard, Uncle Remus would sit in his creaky old rocking chair on the cool verandah, light his pipe and tell his tales to anyone who would care to listen. The children sat with eyes as round as saucers, and if they were good and quiet then they could listen too, and so they heard all about the days when animals strolled around just the same as us folks.

These are some of those stories that Uncle Remus told long ago.

Brer Rabbit
and the Bramble Patch

Brer Fox was having a hard think. He was fed up with that no-good Brer Rabbit strutting about telling the world what a darned clever Rabbit he was. Brer Fox knew he had twice the brains that Rabbit would *ever* have, even if he waited a month of Sundays. He would teach that boastful creature a

thing or too. Yes, sirree, he would teach that Rabbit a lesson he would not forget!

After a while a big smile lit up his face and he went to work. He fetched some black tar and mixed it with turpentine and made himself the strangest little doll you ever did see, and he called that doll his Tar Baby! He put a straw hat on top of her head and very carefully he

picked her up and sat her
down right plumb in the
middle of the road. Then he
hid himself in the bushes to
see what would happen next.

Well, he didn't have long to wait for who should come sauntering down the road, lippity-clippity, clippity-lippity, but that Brer Rabbit just as sassy as a jaybird. Brer Fox, he lay low. Brer Rabbit came closer and closer, looking as if he owned the whole world. Then he caught sight of the Tar Baby and boy, what a surprise he got!

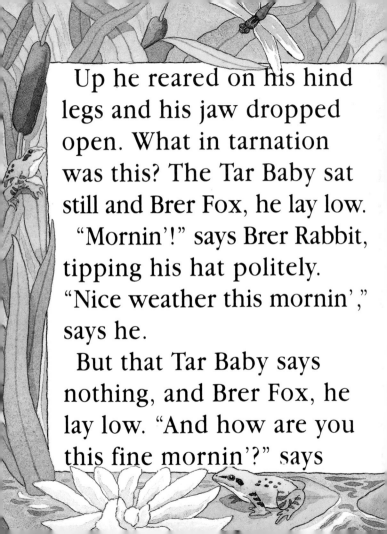

Up he reared on his hind
legs and his jaw dropped
open. What in tarnation
was this? The Tar Baby sat
still and Brer Fox, he lay low.

"Mornin'!" says Brer Rabbit,
tipping his hat politely.
"Nice weather this mornin',"
says he.

But that Tar Baby says
nothing, and Brer Fox, he
lay low. "And how are you
this fine mornin'?" says

Brer Rabbit. That Tar Baby still says nothing, and Brer Fox, he lay low. "What's the matter? You deaf or sumpin'?" says Brer Rabbit. "'Cos if you is, I can holler louder!"

Tar Baby says nothing, and Brer Fox, he lay low.

Well, Brer Rabbit keeps on asking her questions and Tar Baby keeps on saying nothing and that Brer Fox, he just lay low.

"I reckon you're stuck up, that's what I reckon," says Brer Rabbit, getting mad. "I'm gonna teach you some manners," says he. "If you don't take off that hat and wish me howdy, I'm gonna bust your nose!"

Tar Baby says nothing and Brer Fox still lay low, but by now he has a pain in his stomach and an ache in his jaw from trying not to laugh!

Then Brer Rabbit pulls
back his paw and blip! he
swipes that Tar Baby right
on the side of her head!

Well, that was his first big
mistake for now he was well
and truly stuck! Try as he
might he could not pull free.

"If you don't let me go I'm gonna swipe you once more," cries Brer Rabbit, but Tar Baby, she says nothing and Brer Fox, he lay low. So blip! there was his other paw stuck fast. That poor Rabbit started yelling and shouting and soon he had both his hind legs fixed firmly on the sticky Tar Baby. Well, the tears just rolled down Brer Fox's cheeks, and would you believe it but Brer Rabbit only goes and butts that Tar Baby so now his head is stuck fast, too!

Then Brer Fox strolled from the bushes looking just as cool as a cucumber.

"Howdy, Brer Rabbit," says he. "You look kinda stuck up this mornin'!" and then he laughed till his sides ached. "Well, I reckon I got you this time," says Brer

Fox. "You've been struttin' round this neighbourhood like you own the place, puttin' on your fancy airs and graces. Jus' who do you think you is? Nobody asked you to come and get so friendly with this Tar Baby. No, you jus' come along and makes yourself all familiar and sticks yourself all over her, without so much as an if you please."

"Well, you jus' wait there while I goes and lights myself a nice little fire ready for my Brer Rabbit barbecue!"

Now that Brer Rabbit was just as cunning as a barrel-load of crafty monkeys so he thought hard.

"Well, if I've gotta go, I've gotta go and I must say, I'd rather die basted in a good barbecue sauce than be thrown into that bramble patch. Jus' don't throw me in that there bramble patch, Brer Fox!" begged the wily Rabbit.

Brer Fox was surprised to hear this. He had expected Brer Rabbit to be terrified at the thought of being cooked on a fire.

"Well, I guess it's too much trouble to light a fire. Reckon I'm gonna hang you instead," he declared.

"You hang me jus' as high as you like, but please don't fling me in that briar patch!" pleaded Brer Rabbit.

"Shucks, ain't got no string," said Brer Fox. "Guess I'll have to drown you."

"Drown me jus' as deep as you please," cried Brer Fox, "but don't throw me in that there briar patch!"

"No water near here," said Brer Fox. "Ain't nothing for it but to skin you."

"Yes, skin me!" agreed Brer Rabbit. "Scratch out my eyeballs, tear out my hair,

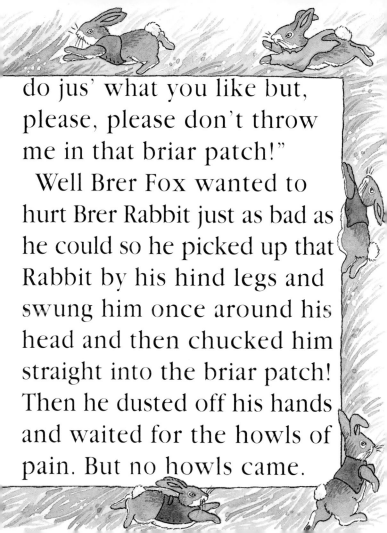

do jus' what you like but, please, please don't throw me in that briar patch!"

Well Brer Fox wanted to hurt Brer Rabbit just as bad as he could so he picked up that Rabbit by his hind legs and swung him once around his head and then chucked him straight into the briar patch! Then he dusted off his hands and waited for the howls of pain. But no howls came.

Just when he thought Brer Rabbit must be good and dead for sure, Brer Fox heard someone calling his name. There was Brer Rabbit sat up on the hill, combing a small speck of tar from his ear, just as bold as you like! Then Brer Fox realised he had been well and truly tricked and he seethed as the Rabbit's voice floated down to him.

"I was born and raised in that briar patch, Brer Fox. Born and raised in that briar patch!"

Brer Rabbit
and the Well

O ne day Brer Rabbit, Brer Fox, Brer Raccoon, Brer Bear and a whole lot of other critters were clearing a new patch of ground.

They had to prepare the land because they wanted to plant a fine crop of corn. It was a hot day, the sun blazed out of a cloudless sky and poor Brer Rabbit soon got tired of working in the fearsome heat.

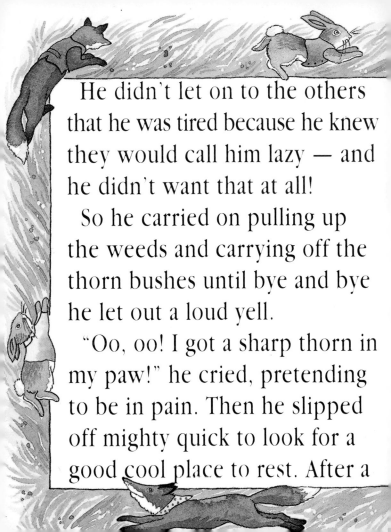

He didn't let on to the others that he was tired because he knew they would call him lazy — and he didn't want that at all!

So he carried on pulling up the weeds and carrying off the thorn bushes until bye and bye he let out a loud yell.

"Oo, oo! I got a sharp thorn in my paw!" he cried, pretending to be in pain. Then he slipped off mighty quick to look for a good cool place to rest. After a

while he came across a well
with a bucket hanging down
into its shady depths.

"That sure looks cool," says
Brer Rabbit. "That looks the very
place for me," and straightaway
he hops into the bucket. Well,
the bucket didn't stay still. No,
sirree. That bucket dropped like
a stone to the bottom of the well.

Well, there hasn't ever been a
beast quite so scared as poor
Brer Rabbit was at that moment.

He knew where he had been a few seconds ago but now he had no idea where he was going! His stomach leapt right up from his belly and landed in his mouth and that ain't a nice place for it to be!

Suddenly the bucket hit the water, blam! Brer Rabbit hunched up good and tight and shivered. He hadn't been expecting this dreadful journey and he wasn't at all sure what might happen next.

Up above in the hot sunshine Brer Fox had stopped work. He always had one eye on what Brer Rabbit was up to and when he saw the rabbit sneak off from the clearing, he downed tools and set off after him. He guessed Brer Rabbit was up to no good but the only way to be sure was to sneak after him and watch. Brer Fox saw Brer Rabbit arrive at the well and stop. He saw him jump in the bucket. Then, lo and behold, he saw him disappear out of sight.

Brer Fox was the most astonished fox you ever set eyes on. He sat in the bushes and thought and thought but whichever way he came at it he could make no sense of it whatsoever.

"Well, if that ain't the darndest thing I ever did see," he muttered to himself. "There has to be a mighty good reason why Brer Rabbit has gone down that well."

Then he clapped his hand to his mouth. "Why, of course!" he cried. "Right down there in that well is where Brer Rabbit

keeps all his money hidden, and if it ain't that, then he's gone and discovered a gold mine, and if it ain't that then I'm sure going to find out just what it is!"

Slowly Brer Fox crept closer to the well and listened. There wasn't a single sound to be heard. Nearer and nearer he crept but still he heard nothing. He reached the well and slowly peered over the edge. Silence.

All this time poor Brer Rabbit was hunched up in that bucket, nearly scared out of his skin. He didn't dare so much as twitch a whisker for fear of the bucket tipping over and spilling him into the cold water. Suddenly a loud voice echoed down the well.

"Howdy, Brer Rabbit! Who are you visiting down there?" called Brer Fox.

"Me?" replied Brer Rabbit, suddenly as cool as a cucumber.

"Why, I'm just fishing, Brer Fox. I was up there working, getting kind of hungry and I thought to myself, 'Why, reckon I'll just go and catch a few fine fish to surprise my friends with for dinner' — and here I am, and here are the fishes."

Brer Fox licked his lips. "Are there many fish down there, Brer Rabbit?" says he.

"Many? *Many*? Are there many grains of sand on the seashore?" replied Brer Rabbit. "Why, this water is so chock full of fish it's almost alive." Brer Fox strained his eyes in the darkness to catch a sight of those wonderful fish.

"Come on down and help me haul them in, Brer Fox. I could do with a hand," said Brer Rabbit.

Brer Fox looked down into the dark shadows. He narrowed his eyes and looked doubtful.

"But how do I get down there, Brer Rabbit? It's awful deep down there," he said, with a shiver.

"Just jump in the bucket you see hanging from the bar, Brer Fox. It will bring you down safe and sound," replied Brer Rabbit, in as sweet and helpful a voice as could be.

Well, Brer Fox could not resist
the thought of all those fishes
jumping and leaping and his
stomach sort of began to growl
and pester him. So up he
jumped into that bucket and
down he went, down, down
into the well. And sure enough,
as he went down, the wily Brer
Rabbit went up. The weight of
the fox in the bucket was pulling
the other bucket up to the top
of the well.

As the two buckets passed one another half way down the well Brer Rabbit began to sing.

'Goodbye, Brer Fox,
take care of your clothes,
for this is the way the world goes.
Some goes up and some goes down,
you'll get to the bottom
all safe and sound.'

Soon the bucket hit the water
and Brer Rabbit reached the top
of the well. Out he jumped and
off he skedaddled back to the
clearing like a shot from a
soldier's musket.

"Hey, folks!" he cried. "That Brer Fox is in the well and muddying up our drinking water!"

The animals kicked up a ruckus like you've never heard and they were off to visit that well in no time.

Brer Rabbit ran on ahead and took great delight in yelling down the well.

'Here comes a man
with a great big gun.
When he hauls you up,
you jump and run!'

Then the animals hauled Brer Fox up out of the well and boxed his ears for dirtying the water. They wouldn't listen to explanations and excuses and pretty soon Brer Fox and Brer Rabbit were back at the clearing, working away as if they had never heard of a well, except that every now and then Brer Rabbit would burst out laughing and that old Brer Fox, he would look as mad, as mad could be.

Brer Rabbit
and the Peanut Patch

B rer Fox wasn't much of a gardener; ask anybody, they'll all tell you the same thing. But one year he decided it was high time he got the hang of growing things for himself and he decided he would plant a peanut patch. Well, once he'd made his mind up to do it he was raring to go.

"I'm going to plant me some peanuts," he declared to the

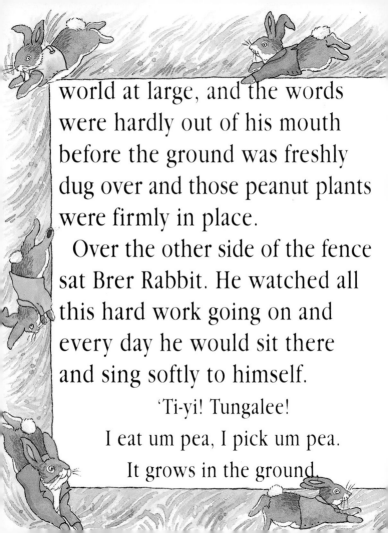

world at large, and the words
were hardly out of his mouth
before the ground was freshly
dug over and those peanut plants
were firmly in place.

Over the other side of the fence
sat Brer Rabbit. He watched all
this hard work going on and
every day he would sit there
and sing softly to himself.

'Ti-yi! Tungalee!
I eat um pea, I pick um pea.
It grows in the ground.

it grows so free.

Ti-yi! good peanut pea!'

Sure enough, when those peanuts had grown big and ripe that Brer Rabbit, he helped himself just as sassy as you please. Every morning Brer Fox went down to his peanut patch all excited to inspect his crop and when he discovered that somebody had been scrabbling in and out of the plants he grew mighty mad.

He had his suspicions about who the culprit might be but that wily Brer Rabbit was careful to cover up his tracks each day and so Brer Fox was never able to hunt him down.

One day Brer Fox was inspecting his beautiful peanut patch. He was mighty proud of that patch, and as cautious and protective as if each one of those plants was his own little child. He would never have believed the pleasure he got from raising those tender green shoots from seed. As he strolled by the fence that surrounded his garden he suddenly spied a small hole close to the ground.

"Blessed if that ain't where the little varmint who is stealing my peanuts gets through," he said to himself. Off he went to find some rope and, pulling a hickory sapling down to the ground, he tied that rope in a slip knot around the branch and pretty soon had made a darned good trap.

The next day ole Brer Rabbit came sashaying down the road, and when he reached Brer Fox's fence he bent down and wriggled through the hole. Sure enough, the rope slipped tight around his legs, the sapling flew up in the air and there hung Brer Rabbit, 'twixt heaven and earth! There he swung back and forth; one minute scared he was going to fall, the next minute scared he *wasn't* going to fall.

As he swung to and fro he tried to think up a tale to tell Brer Fox but before he had managed to come up with a story that he was perfectly satisfied with, who should he hear ambling down the road but Brer Bear.

"Howdy, Brer Bear!" cries Brer Rabbit. Brer Bear's huge head slowly turned from side to side.

"Whassat? Whoosair?" he said.

"I'm up here, Brer Bear," called Brer Rabbit.

"Look up in the hickory tree." The big bear raised his head and was astonished to see Brer Rabbit hanging upside down, just as calm and contented as you like.

"Howdy, Brer Rabbit," he said. "And how are you this fine bee-buzzing morning?"

"Fair to middling, Brer Bear," replies Brer Rabbit. "Fair to middling."

Brer Bear stood and stared.

"Brer Rabbit?" says Brer Bear, scratching his head. "Would you mind telling me just what in the Sam Hill you is doing up in that there tree?"

Brer Rabbit smiled down at

him in an upside down sort of way and replied, "I'm earning a dollar a minute, Brer Bear."

"A dollar a minute!" spluttered Brer Bear. "That's pretty good going, Brer Rabbit."

"Sure is, and all I have to do is keep the crows out of Brer Fox's peanut patch."

Brer Rabbit looked at Brer Bear and Brer Bear looked at Brer Rabbit. After a while Brer Rabbit spoke again.

"Say, I don't suppose you want the chance to earn a dollar a minute? I only ask because I know what a big family you have to feed what with all those children of yours. Gee, it must be mighty difficult to fill those little mouths."

Brer Bear nodded ruefully. "You never said a truer word, brother," he agreed. Then he looked up at the hickory tree. "Do you reckon I could do it?" he asked.

"Why, I reckon you was born to make a scarecrow," replied Brer Rabbit encouragingly, and soon he had told the bear exactly what to do. Brer Bear pulled down the sapling with one mighty paw and had soon freed Brer Rabbit from the rope.

Then placing both his huge feet back in the loop, he let go of the whippy tree and soon he was hanging upside down just exactly the same as Brer Rabbit had been two minutes earlier.

Brer Rabbit looked mighty happy to be down on the ground once again. He jumped twice in the air then skedaddled off to Brer Fox's house leaving Brer Bear swinging in the wind.

"Brer Fox! Brer Fox!" cried out

Brer Rabbit when he reached the porch. "Come on out and I'll show you the rascal who's been stealing your precious peanuts!"

Out bowled Brer Fox, stout walking stick in hand, and up the road they both ran, lickety-split.

"So that's your lowdown game, is it?" shouted Brer Fox when he caught sight of Brer Bear hanging in the wind. "You're the varmint who's been at my peanuts!"

Brer Bear had no time to explain that he was acting as a scarecrow to keep the birds off the peanut patch. Old Brer Fox didn't want to hear. He just set to with his stick and caught him a crack across his broad brown back

"Oo! Ow!" wailed poor Brer Bear. "I was — ow! — looking after — oo! — your peanuts, Brer Fox!"

"Nibbling my best shoots!" BLAM! "Scrabbling up their little roots!" BLIM! "You call that looking after my plants?" BLAM! "You great loafer!" shouted Brer Fox as he worked hard with his stick. "Well, I'll know not to come to you when I need help with my gardening!" he cried.

Brer Rabbit nearly split his sides laughing but when he saw that Brer Fox had finished punishing Brer Bear and was cutting him free from the trap, he hightailed out of there for he was no fool, that rabbit.

He hid in a mud hole by the side of the road with just his eyes sticking out. Bye and bye Brer Bear came limping down the road. He spied these two round eyes and he stopped.

"Howdy, Brer Frog," he said. "You didn't happen to see Brer Rabbit coming down this way?"

"Knee-deep, knee-deep! He just went by a few minutes ago," replied that cunning Brer Rabbit in a croaky frog-like voice.

Brer Bear ground his teeth at the thought of how foolish he had been and off he lumbered down the road, muttering and moaning. And that Brer Rabbit jumped out of the mud hole, dried himself off in the sun, and sauntered off home to his family, same as any man.

Brer Rabbit
and the Turtle Race

It was springtime and everyone felt mighty glad to be alive. Brer Rabbit felt especially full of the joys of spring as he nibbled the tender, juicy shoots in the peanut patch. He was smart and always the first to find the freshest leaves! But one day he met his match and then he didn't look quite so happy, I can tell you.

One fine spring day as Brer Rabbit ran lippity clippity up the road he passed by old Brer Turtle.

"Good job you ain't in no particular hurry," scoffed Brer Rabbit as he raced by.

"I could go as fast as you if I wanted, *which* I don't," replied Brer Turtle, calm as you please. Brer Rabbit skidded to a halt and walked back towards the Turtle.

"Say *what*?" he exclaimed, disbelievingly. "Why, you're so slow that by the time you get to the shops, they've drawn down the shutters, locked the doors and gone home to tea."

Well, before long they fell to arguing about who was the fastest and, blow me, if ole Brer Turtle didn't issue a challenge right there and then.

"I ain't gonna argue the toss no more," says he. "Tucked away out of sight in a chink of my chimney at home there's a fifty dollar bill says I'll beat you fair and square." Brer Rabbit could not believe his ears. *Easy* money!

"And *I* have fifty dollars says you're gonna kiss my heels, Brer Turtle!" says he, with a delighted grin.

"Why, I could sew grass seeds as I run along and by the time *you* pass that way, they'd be grown tall enough to give you a good meal!"

Well, ole Brer Turtle was
having none of it and
calmly repeated that he was
sure he could beat Brer
Rabbit in a race. With a
pitying shake of his head,
Brer Rabbit agreed to take
part in the challenge and so
it was all arranged.
   Brer Buzzard was
summoned to be the judge
and Brer Bear was given the
important job of firing the

starting pistol. A five mile
course was measured off
with posts to mark the end
of every mile. Brer Rabbit
was going to run along the
road but for some reason
Brer Turtle decided he
would race through the
wood. Folks said he was
plumb crazy to choose
such a course, but that Brer
Turtle, he knew what he
was doing, all right.

Brer Rabbit began to train like a professional. He jogged up and down the dusty road for four hours every day. He skipped, he lifted weights, he wore a bright pink track suit and drank fizzy water.

And how did ole Brer Turtle train for the big event? Well, he lay in his swamp and dozed. Now Brer Turtle had a big family. He had a wife and three children, all the spitting image of their father. You could put them under a magnifying glass to tell them apart and even then there'd be no cast iron guarantee you'd get it right.

So Brer Turtle quietly snoozed in the mud and Brer Rabbit pumped iron until his muscles felt ready to pop.

The day of the race dawned clear and bright and even before sun up, Brer Turtle and his family had got themselves into position. Brer Turtle had a plan, a very good plan. He had thought of a way to beat that boastful rabbit and teach him a lesson once and for all. His family had their instructions and knew just what to do. Brer Turtle's wife waited by the starting post, and his three children each waited behind the next three posts, and where was Brer Turtle? Why, hiding in the woods near the very last post of all, of course!

Soon a big crowd had gathered to watch the race and Miss Meadows and her girls were there to cheer them both on.

Brer Rabbit jogged at the starting line as Brer Buzzard called, "Take your marks!"

"Ready when you are," cried Mrs Turtle and she sounded just exactly like Brer Turtle.

"Ready, steady, go!" cried Brer Bear and they were off! Brer Rabbit raced down the road past the hooting crowd, but ole Mrs Turtle scuttled off into the wood.

When Brer Rabbit reached the first mile post he called out, "You there, Brer Turtle?" and Brer Turtle's eldest child crawled out onto the road and said, "Right behind you, Brer Rabbit." Then Brer Rabbit set off again like a steam train and young Master Turtle went home.

Soon Brer Rabbit reached the next mile post.

"You there, Brer Turtle?" he said. And out crawled Brer Turtle's middle child.

"Sure am," said she, and crawled off home. But Brer Rabbit just carried on steaming down the road.

The same thing happened at the next mile post and this time Brer Turtle's youngest little 'un crawled out, put in an appearance and went home.

Panting breathlessly, Brer Rabbit loped along the final mile. "Just how is that Turtle managing to keep up?" he kept thinking.

Soon the finish line was in sight and Brer Rabbit could see Brer Buzzard hovering overhead ready to announce the winner. But he didn't see Brer Turtle come out of the woods and hide behind the line!

"Gimme the money, Brer Buzzard! I won the race!" hollered Brer Rabbit and Miss Meadows and the girls began to laugh and laugh.

Then blow me if that Brer Turtle didn't rise up on his little hind legs and say, "If you'll just give me time to catch my breath, ladies and gents, I think I'll just pocket that money myself!" And tying the purse around his neck and before Brer Rabbit could engage his brain to talk, he skedaddled off home without so much as a backward glance!

Fishing for
the Moon

From time to time all the animals would get together and try to enjoy each other's company. They would ignore the fact that they had had their disagreements and Brer Rabbit would make up his mind once and for all that he was going to quit his bad ways and cause no more trouble around the neighbourhood.

But sooner or later the time would come when Brer Rabbit began to feel kind of twitchy. The more

contented and placid the
other animals seemed to
be, the more bad-tempered
and restless he became.

As the days rolled eacefully by, he lay in the ong grass and kicked irritably at the buzzing gnats. He chewed peevishly at the melon stalks and scuffed his feet in the dust. He had a home and a full tummy but it seemed to him as if something was still missing.

One night after supper he was strolling around

wondering how to fill the hours before bedtime when he bumped into ole Brer Turtle. They shook hands solemnly then sat down on the side of the road to chat. Pretty soon the talk came round to tales of the old days and how they hooted with laughter as the memories flooded back. Bye and bye Brer Rabbit gave a great sigh.

"I gotta confession to make, Brer Turtle," said he. "I miss those good ole, bad ole days."

Brer Turtle scratched his jaw gloomily. "Know just what you mean, Brer Rabbit," said he "We sure had some fun back then."

"I gotta mighty strong urge to have some fun again, Brer Turtle," said Brer Rabbit meaningfully.

"I got that urge too, Brer Rabbit," replied Brer Turtle and soon they were happily hatching a plot.

"In the morning I'll go see Brer Fox, Brer Wolf and Brer Bear," announced Brer Rabbit. "I'll invite them to meet us down at the millpond tomorrow evening and we'll have a little fishing frolic. I'll do all the talking and you just say 'yes'!" Brer Turtle chortled with glee. "Happy to oblige, Brer Rabbit," he said. "Happy to oblige."

Brer Rabbit sauntered off home feeling cheerful, relaxed and more at peace with the world than he had done for weeks.

The next day he sent word of the fishing party to Brer Fox, Brer Wolf and Brer Bear and they were thrilled.

"What a fine idea!" said Brer Fox, clasping his paws under his chin.

"Now why didn't I think of that!" said Brer Wolf admiringly.

Hiding a sly grin, Brer Rabbit loped off to Miss Meadows' house and invited her and the girls to join them. So it was that they all met up on the edge of the millpond later that night.

Brer Bear carried a landing net, Brer Fox had a hook and line and Brer Turtle held a large box of wriggling maggots to use as bait.

Brer Turtle took great delight in shaking the box at Miss Meadows and the girls as they squealed with horror. "I'm gonna fish for mud-cats," said Brer Bear. "And I'm gonna fish for horneyheads," decided Brer Wolf. Brer Fox smiled kinda slow and winked at Brer Turtle. "Reckon I'm gonna catch me some suckers," he said quietly. With that he prepared to cast his hook into the water. Suddenly he started and the eyes nearly popped out of his head. He clutched his pole and scratched his head in bewilderment as he stared down into the depths of the pond. The girls grew uneasy and presently Miss Meadows called out, "Lawks, Brer Rabbit, just what have you seen in there?"

Brer Rabbit rubbed his chin and stared hard at the pond. Miss Meadows nervously gathered up her skirts. "I'm most monstrous scared of snakes," she quavered. "Tell me it ain't snakes, Brer Rabbit!" Brer Rabbit shook his head and sighed. "Well," he said, "we might all just as well turn around and go home for there'll be no fishing tonight.

Then Brer Turtle scrambled to the edge of the pond and peered over. He shook his head. "Well I never!" he said, most astonished. "Lawks a mercy!"

"Now don't be scared, ladies," reassured Brer Rabbit as he laid a comforting paw on Miss Meadows' arm. "Accidents will happen come what may and there's nothing at all for you to worry about." Miss Meadows looked very worried. "There has been something of a mishap and I'm very much afraid that the moon has gone and fallen in the water."

Everyone rushed to the water's edge and looked in and sure enough, there lay the moon quivering at the bottom of the pool.

"Well, well," said Brer Fox.

"Mighty bad, mighty bad," sighed Brer Wolf.

"Tut, tut, tut," tutted Brer Bear. Then the ladies looked in and Miss Meadows squawked, "Ain't that just too much?" Brer Rabbit shrugged his shoulders and spoke. "Well, you can all hum and haw but unless we get that moon out of the pond, there'll be no fishing for any of us tonight."

Brer Rabbit winked at Brer Turtle. "And if you don't believe me," he added, "you can just ask Brer Turtle."

"It's true sure enough," agreed Brer Turtle, nodding his head energetically. The animals decided at once that there was nothing for it but to take that moon from out of the pond.

"But how shall we do it?" asked Brer Bear. Then Brer

Rabbit closed his eyes tight and pretended to think hard. "I reckon the best way out of this here difficulty is to run round to ole Mr Mud Turtle and borrow his large fishing net. We're gonna have to drag that moon from the pond."

"Mr Mud Turtle is a close relation of mine," added Brer Turtle. "Fact is, I call him Unc Muck!"

So Brer Rabbit ran off to fetch the net and Brer Turtle filled the time by telling everyone that he believed this sort of thing had happened before and he had heard tell that if someone succeeded in pulling the moon out of a pond then they would also pull out a pot full of money at the same time.

Then Brer Bear, Brer Fox

and Brer Wolf grew mighty excited. "Seeing as how Brer Rabbit's been so good as to run and fetch the net, we'll do the job of hauling the moon from the water," said Brer Fox hastily.

So they all three waded into the pond and Brer Fox took hold of one end of the net, Brer Wolf took hold of the other, and Brer Bear followed behind.

They dragged the net
through the water and
hauled it up. No moon!
They made another haul.
Still no moon!

Soon they were right out in the middle of the pond and here the water was deep and cold. It ran in Brer Fox's ears and he shook his head. It ran in Brer Wolf's nose and he snorted. It ran in Brer Bear's mouth and he choked. They were so busy that they didn't notice the pond bottom suddenly dropped away from under their feet!

One by one their heads disappeared and bobbed up again as the poor animals thrashed the water with

their arms. They flailed about so much it was a wonder they didn't empty the pond of all its water!

Soon they reached the bank and you never saw such poor bedraggled creatures in all your life!

Miss Meadows and the girls tried to hide their snickering but they didn't make a very good job of it.

Brer Turtle was crying with laughter so bad that he had to pretend he had a fly in his eye so as not to cause offence.

Brer Rabbit gallantly helped Brer Bear, Fox and Wolf up onto dry land and slowly looked them up and down. "I think you better go home and get into some dry clothes, gentlemen," he said, acting all concerned. "Maybe we could try and catch the moon another night. You know, I'm sure you'll get lucky sooner or later because I hear tell that the moon will only bite the hook if you use fools as bait and I reckon that's the only way *you'll* catch her."

Brer Fox, Brer Bear and Brer Wolf looked at him blankly as the water dripped off their noses and they didn't see Brer Rabbit wink at Brer Turtle, or Brer Turtle wink back at him!

One day Brer Wolf was on his way home after a good day's fishing. He sauntered along with a string of fish over his shoulder when all of a sudden Miss Partridge flew out of the bushes right in front of his nose. She squawked so angrily that Brer Wolf figured she must be trying to lure him away from her nest of young 'uns.

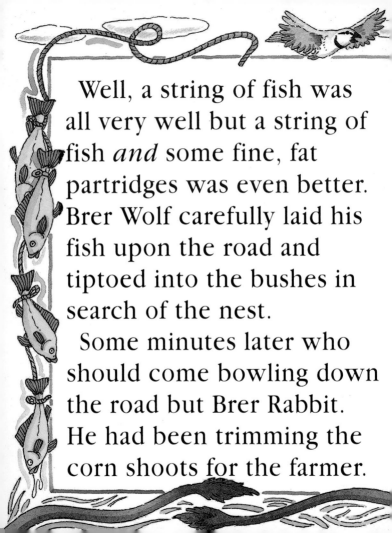

Well, a string of fish was all very well but a string of fish *and* some fine, fat partridges was even better. Brer Wolf carefully laid his fish upon the road and tiptoed into the bushes in search of the nest.

Some minutes later who should come bowling down the road but Brer Rabbit. He had been trimming the corn shoots for the farmer.

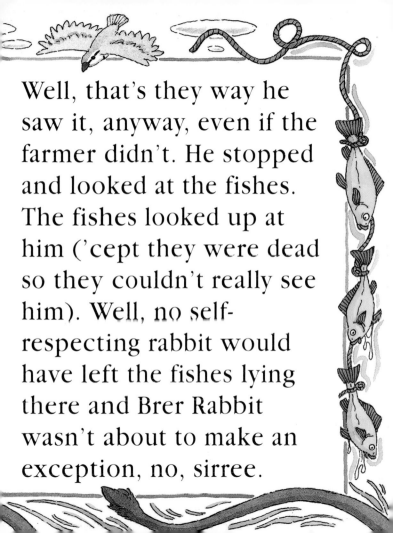

Well, that's they way he saw it, anyway, even if the farmer didn't. He stopped and looked at the fishes. The fishes looked up at him ('cept they were dead so they couldn't really see him). Well, no self-respecting rabbit would have left the fishes lying there and Brer Rabbit wasn't about to make an exception, no, sirree.

Off he ran with the fishes over his shoulder and when Brer Wolf returned there was nothing on the ground but a fishy-smelling damp patch.

Brer Wolf pretty soon worked out what had happened. It could be no-one else but that pesky Brer Rabbit! But when he got to Brer Rabbit's house and put the matter to him, Brer Rabbit flatly denied it. Brer Wolf insisted. Brer Rabbit disagreed. Brer Wolf persisted. Brer Rabbit protested. At last Brer Rabbit looked him in the eye.

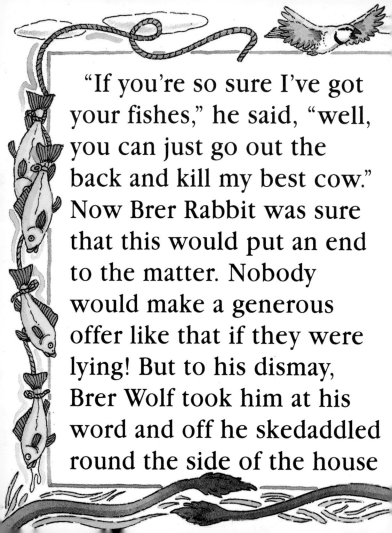

"If you're so sure I've got your fishes," he said, "well, you can just go out the back and kill my best cow." Now Brer Rabbit was sure that this would put an end to the matter. Nobody would make a generous offer like that if they were lying! But to his dismay, Brer Wolf took him at his word and off he skedaddled round the side of the house in search of Brer Rabbit's best cow. Wasn't long before he found her and he killed her on the spot.

Brer Rabbit was mighty sore to see his plan backfire but he wasn't beaten yet.

"Don't you worry, you rabs," he told his wide-eyed children. "Ain't nobody going to take that meat away from us." Then he had an idea.

Brer Wolf had been arrested by the police some days earlier and ever since had been greatly afraid of a repeat performance.

"Police! It's the police, Brer Wolf!" cried Brer Rabbit at the top of his voice. "You better run and hide and I'll stay here and look after the cow until you get back." Well, you couldn't see Brer Wolf for dust.

Quickly Brer Rabbit set to work. He skinned the cow and salted the hide. He cut the meat into pieces and all his little children happily stowed it away in the smoke-house.

Then Brer Rabbit took the cow's tail and stuck one end in the ground. He allowed himself a quick chortle at the sight of it then wiped the smile of his face and called out loudly.

"The police have gone, Brer Wolf," he cried. "But you better come quick! Something strange is happening here. Your cow is going under the ground!"

Out from the bushes ran
Brer Wolf and his jaw
sagged as he beheld the
scene before him. There
stood Brer Rabbit gripping
on to the end of the cow's
tail as if his very life
depended on it.

"Give me a hand, Brer
Wolf!" he cried, kind of
panic-stricken. "This here
cow is trying to get deeper
underground!"

Brer Wolf grabbed hold of the tail and pulled with all his might. He pulled and pulled and then — pop! — out came the tail from the ground!

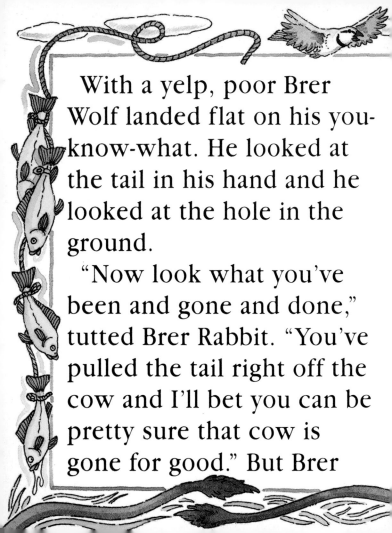

With a yelp, poor Brer Wolf landed flat on his you-know-what. He looked at the tail in his hand and he looked at the hole in the ground.

"Now look what you've been and gone and done," tutted Brer Rabbit. "You've pulled the tail right off the cow and I'll bet you can be pretty sure that cow is gone for good." But Brer

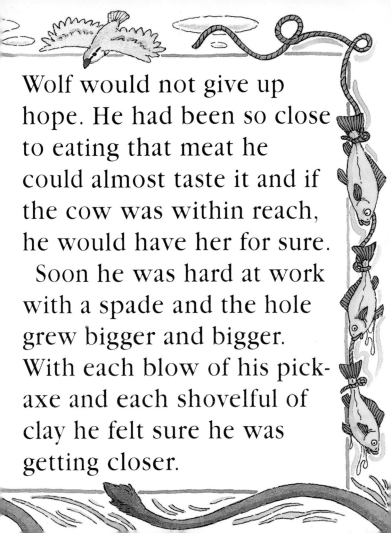

Wolf would not give up hope. He had been so close to eating that meat he could almost taste it and if the cow was within reach, he would have her for sure.

Soon he was hard at work with a spade and the hole grew bigger and bigger. With each blow of his pick-axe and each shovelful of clay he felt sure he was getting closer.

Brer Rabbit sat back in his rocking chair and smiled happily as his children frolicked around him.

"He diggy, diggy, diggy, but no meat there!" he laughed. "He diggy, diggy, diggy, but no meat there!"

Brer Rabbit
and the Riding Horse

Brer Fox was strutting around the neighbourhood feeling mighty pleased with himself. He had made good and sure that everyone, but *everyone*, had heard all about how he had tricked poor old Brer Rabbit with the sticky tar baby. Certainly Miss Meadows and her girls thought it was the funniest thing they had ever heard!

The next time Brer Rabbit came a-visiting, their stifled giggles quite ruined the conversation. Brer Rabbit drank his tea just as polite as you would wish and said not a word. But by and by, he put down his cup.

"Ladies," he announced. "Brer Fox was my daddy's riding horse for a good thirty years," then he bid them good-day and left.

Next day Brer Fox came a-calling and Miss Meadows told him what Brer Rabbit had said. Brer Fox grew quite red with anger then, composing himself, said,

"Ladies, I'm gonna make that Brer Rabbit eat his words and spit 'em out right here where you can see 'em!" and with that he headed straight for Brer Rabbit's house.

Well, Brer Rabbit wasn't at all surprised to hear Brer Fox banging on his front door but he kept as quiet as a weevil. Brer Fox hammered and hammered, blam! blam! blam! but still Brer Rabbit laid low.

Finally Brer Rabbit called out in a quavering voice, "Is that you, Brer Fox? Please run and fetch the doctor. I ate some parsley this morning and it sure is disagreeing with me. I feel proper poorly!"

"Well, isn't that a shame," says Brer Fox. "I just came from Miss Meadows and the girls and seems they've invited you to their party.

Wouldn't be worth having a party if you couldn't be there, they said."

Then they set to arguing about whether or not Brer Rabbit was well enough to go to the party. Brer Rabbit says he can't walk there, so Brer Fox says he'll carry him. Brer Rabbit says he'll drop him so to make sure he'll be safe he must ride on the Fox's back.

Eventually after much humming and hawing Brer Fox agrees. Then Brer Rabbit says he can't ride without a saddle and Brer Fox says he'll fetch a saddle. Then Brer Rabbit says he'll fall off unless he has a bridle to hold onto and Brer Fox agrees to fetch a bridle. Oh, but it has to have blinkers, says Brer Rabbit, quite firmly.

And so Brer Fox says he'll fetch blinkers — but on one condition. Brer Rabbit cannot ride him all the way to Miss Meadows. Oh, no! That would never do. Brer Rabbit must get off and walk so no-one can see Brer Fox wearing a saddle. And so Brer Rabbit agrees and then that's all settled and off runs Brer Fox to get the saddle and bridle.

With a big smile on his face, that Brer Rabbit gets ready for the party. He combs his hair, waxes his moustache and soon looks fine and dandy.

Up comes Brer Fox in saddle and bridle and up jumps Brer Rabbit as if he was a born horseman!

And so all was settled and off they set down the road and by and by Brer Fox felt Brer Rabbit raise one of his feet.

"I'm just shortening my left stirrup," explained the Rabbit. Soon Brer Rabbit raised his other foot.

"Just shortening my right stirrup," he told Brer Fox, but *would* you believe it, that wily Rabbit had fitted himself with spurs and now he was ready to have some fun! As they drew close to Miss Meadows' house, Brer Fox stopped, for he wanted Brer Rabbit to get off and walk, but Brer Rabbit just smiled and stuck his spurs into Brer Fox's flanks.

My, how that Fox shifted! Past the house they galloped, then turned and raced back again.

Brer Rabbit coolly dismounted and with a dramatic flourish hitched Brer Fox to the rail in front of the verandah. Casually brushing the dust from his trousers, he shook Miss Meadows and the girls politely by the hand, sat himself down and lit a fine large cigar.

"Ladies, didn't I tell you Brer Fox was our family's

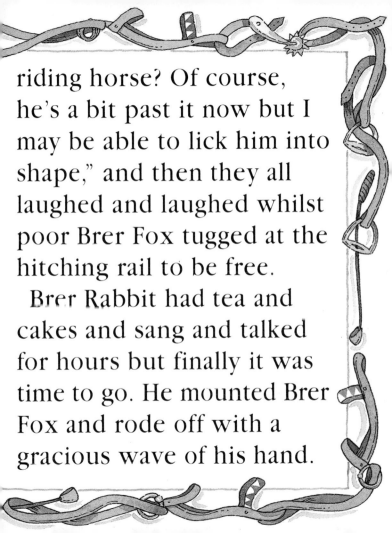

riding horse? Of course, he's a bit past it now but I may be able to lick him into shape," and then they all laughed and laughed whilst poor Brer Fox tugged at the hitching rail to be free.

Brer Rabbit had tea and cakes and sang and talked for hours but finally it was time to go. He mounted Brer Fox and rode off with a gracious wave of his hand.

Off he went down the road but as soon as they were out of sight Brer Fox went wild. He bucked and pranced, snorted and cavorted but he might just as well have wrestled with his own shadow for all the good it did him. Brer Rabbit dug in those spurs and yanked on that bridle and soon Brer Fox was as mad as a bee-stung bear.

Then Brer Fox lay down on the ground and rolled on his back and in no time at all Brer Rabbit was off and running. Brer Fox chased him and very near got him, too, but Brer Rabbit made straight for a hollow tree and was soon safe and sound inside. Brer Fox lay down outside the hole and did some thinking Soon Brer Buzzard came flopping along.

"You stand guard over this hole, Brer Buzzard," said Brer Fox, "and don't you let that pesky Brer Rabbit escape. I'm gonna get my big axe!"

When Brer Fox had gone, Brer Rabbit called out of the hole, "Brer Fox! Brer Fox! I know you're out there," said he, "and I don't care. I just wish Brer Buzzard was here, that's all."

Then Brer Buzzard tried to sound like Brer Fox.

"Why do you want Brer Buzzard?" he asked.

"Oh, nothing in particular," says Brer Rabbit. "It's just that there's the biggest grey squirrel in here and if Brer Buzzard was to come to this little hole round the other side of the tree, I'm sure I could chase that little varmint straight to him."

"You drive him out," says Brer Buzzard, all eager, "and I'll make sure that Brer Buzzard gets him!"

Then Brer Rabbit kicks up a racket and Brer Buzzard rushes round to the back of the tree and licketty-spit, out races Brer Rabbit from his hole at the front of the tree and doesn't stop running till he's safe and sound in his own home!

Brer Rabbit's Good Children

No matter what else you might say about Brer Rabbit's children (and some people had plenty to say, such as "pesky little critters" and "darned wabbits", but we have no time to go into that now), no matter what else you might say, those rabbits were mighty careful to do just as they were told by their mother and father.

When ole man rabbit says
"scoot", they scoot, and
when ole Mrs Rabbit says
"scat", they scat. They kept
their clothes clean and they
always washed behind their
ears. They were good little
rabbits.

And it was a good thing that these little rabbits were good and always did as they were told because one day something happened when if they *hadn't* been good, well, that would have been the end of them, for sure. This is how it came about.

Ole Brer Fox was passing by Brer Rabbit's house and he decided he would call in and pass the time of day.

But when he knocked on the door, a little voice explained that his mother and father were not at home. "My mammy is helping old Mrs Buzzard with her quilting and my pappy is inspecting Brer Turtle's cabbage patch," he said. "Hmm!" thought Brer Fox. "*Inspecting* it, is he? More like raiding it, I'd say," but he didn't say anything.

Brer Fox peeked through the window and when he saw the fat little rabbits playing hide and seek his mouth fair began to water.

He tapped on the glass and the little rabbits froze.

"Let me in," called Brer Fox in a soft, wheedling voice, "and I'll just sit and wait for your ole daddy to return." Soon Brer Fox was sitting in a corner of the room and watching the little rabbits' noses twitching. "Don't mind me," he said. "You all just carry on with your games."

But somehow the rabbits had lost interest in playing and they huddled together, their ears quivering. Brer Fox badly wanted to gobble them up but he dare not do it without some sort of good excuse. Bye and bye he saw a big stalk of sugar cane leaning against the wall. "I sure am hungry," says he. "Break me off a piece of that cane, will you?"

Well, those rabbits were brought up to be polite to visitors so they tried to do as he asked. But as much as they wrestled and sweated over that sugar cane, they could not break a piece off.

Now Brer Fox knew there isn't much else tougher in the world than sugar cane and he hoped that the rabbits would fail, for then he would have an excuse to eat them. Those little rabbits pushed and pulled but the sugar cane didn't even bend.

"Hurry up, you rabs!" cried Brer Fox. "I don't like to be kept waiting." Just then the

rabbits heard a little bird
singing on the rooftop.

"*Take your toofies
and gnaw it.
Take your toofies and saw it.
Saw it and gnaw it
And then you can break it!*"

Then the rabbits set to
with their sharp little teeth
and in no time at all they
laid a fine piece of juicy
sugar cane at ole Brer Fox's
feet.

Brer Fox looked pretty sick when he saw that his crafty plan had failed, and as he chewed on the cane his mind worked overtime to come up with another way to trick them. Then he caught sight of a sieve hanging on the wall.

"Here, rabbits!" he said. "I'm mighty thirsty. Take this sieve and fetch me some water from the spring."

Then the rabbits ran down
and dipped the sieve into
the water, but to their
dismay the water trickled
straight out of the holes
and all over the ground.

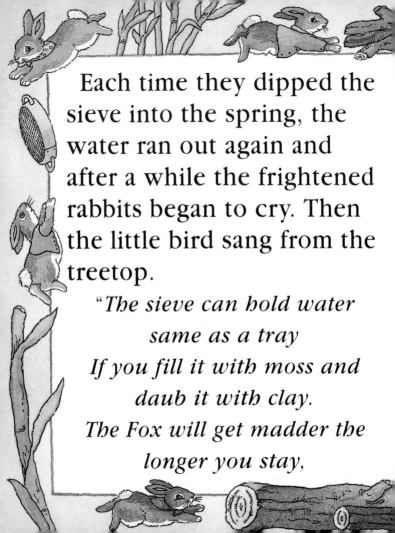

Each time they dipped the sieve into the spring, the water ran out again and after a while the frightened rabbits began to cry. Then the little bird sang from the treetop.

"The sieve can hold water same as a tray
If you fill it with moss and daub it with clay.
The Fox will get madder the longer you stay,

Fill it with moss and daub it with clay."

Up jumped the rabbits and they did just as the bird had told them to do. Soon the sieve did indeed hold water just as good as a tray. They carried the water back to ole Brer Fox, but when he saw that they had succeeded he was mighty mad and he ground his teeth in a regular temper.

Then he spied a large log lying in the woodpile.

"Right, you rabs," he said just a touch testily. "I'm feeling kind of chilly. Put that log on the fire and warm me up."

The rabbits put their paws on that log and heaved and pushed with all their might, but would that log budge? No, sirree, for it was a mighty big log. Just then they heard the bird sing.

"Spit on your paws and tug it and toll it.

Get behind it and push it and pole it.

Spit on your paws and rock it and roll it."

So the rabbits set to and as Brer Fox gnashed his teeth, they finally got that log on the fire. Just then who should walk in but Brer Rabbit and his wife, and they were pretty surprised to see old Brer Fox sitting there looking as black as thunder. My, how the little rabs were pleased to see them, though, and they skipped for joy. Then Brer

Fox grinned sheepishly, for he saw that his game was up. He got to his feet and began to make his excuses to leave. Brer Rabbit only needed to take one look at his jittery little children to realise that something had been going on and he narrowed his eyes. "Why, do stay and have tea with us, Brer Fox. I get quite lonesome these long nights."

But Brer Fox shuffled to the door and was off.

"Thank you kindly, Brer Rabbit," says he, "but not this time — no, not this time."

How Miss Cow
was Milked

Late one afternoon Brer Rabbit was on his way home after a good day rooting about in ole Brer Fox's peanut patch. As the long shadows stretched out across the dusty ground he stopped and yawned.

"What wouldn't I give for something to drink," he said to himself. Just then he spied Miss Cow grazing peacefully in the meadow.

Now he knew that Miss Cow would not give him some of her milk. No, sirree. He had asked her once before and had received a less than satisfactory reply. So he would just have to think of a plan. "Howdy, Sis Cow," said Brer Rabbit, as he leaned over the fence.

"Why, howdy, Brer Rabbit," replied Miss Cow

and she carried on chewing the sweet grass.

"How's life treating you these days, Sis Cow?" says he, all polite and respectful.

"Why, fair to middling," replied Miss Cow, and she looked at him with her big brown eyes. "And how's life treating you?"

"Oh, no complaints," said Brer Rabbit. "No complaints at all."

"How's Brer Bull getting on?" asked Brer Rabbit.

"Oh, so-so, I guess," said Miss Cow. Then Brer Rabbit cleared his throat. "There are some mighty fine persimmons in that there tree, Sis Cow," says he. "I sure would like to taste some of that fruit."

Miss Cow looked up at the branches above her head.

"How are you going to

reach them?" she asked.

Brer Rabbit looked back at her, unblinkingly. "Well, I wondered if you might help me out there," he said. "If you butted the tree you could shake them to the ground." Miss Cow was happy to oblige. She ran up to the persimmon tree and banged her horns hard against the trunk — *blam*! But not a single fruit fell down. Then Miss Cow took several steps backwards, lowered her head and ran against the tree at full speed — *blim*! Not a persimmon budged from the branch. And it was hardly surprising, for those persimmons were as green as grass and nowhere near ripe enough to fall — as Brer Rabbit knew full well. Then Miss Cow backed up again.

This time she hit the tree so hard — *kerblam*! that it was a wonder she didn't knock herself out on the spot. But when she came to step away from the tree she found she couldn't move.

One of her horns had stuck in the tree and she was caught fast! She couldn't move forward, she couldn't move backward, Miss Cow was well and truly there to stay. Then Brer Rabbit smiled to himself for his plan had worked perfectly.

"Help me out, Brer Rabbit," begged Miss Cow.

"*I* won't be much help to

you, Sis Cow," he called out, "but I'll run and tell Brer Bull, if you like."

Then off he ran down the road. It wasn't long before he returned — but who was this accompanying him? It certainly didn't look like big Brer Bull! It was Brer Rabbit's missus and all Brer Rabbit's little chilluns and every one of them held a milking pail.

The big chilluns had big
pails and the little chilluns
had little pails and pretty
soon they were clustered
so tight around Miss Cow
you could hardly see hide
nor hair of her.

Ole Brer Rabbit calmly sat down on his three legged milking stool and filled pail after pail with sweet warm milk and pretty soon he had milked Miss Cow dry. Then he stood up and grinned.

"I realised you were gonna be stuck in that there tree all night and I figured you'd be pretty sore carrying all that milk, so I thought I'd help you out. Kind of a good deed, you might say." Then he skedaddled off down the road after his family and their clinking milk pails. Miss Cow was just beside herself with rage. All night long she tried to free herself but it wasn't until daybreak that she finally tugged her horn out of the trunk. The first thing she did was to eat some grass and fill her empty stomach.

Then she stopped to think how she might get her own back on that pesky Brer Rabbit. She reckoned he would be coming along that way soon so she stuck her horn back in the tree trunk. She had got a trick up her sleeve for sure. But that cunning Brer Rabbit returned bright and early and he saw Miss Cow push her horn back in the hole.

"Hold your horses, Sis Cow," he said to himself. "Looks to me as if you took one mouthful of grass too many. If you want to play tricks on me, you gotta be quicker than that." Then he came loping up the road whistling a merry tune and looking the very picture of innocence. "Morning, Sis Cow," he said, "and how are you this fine morning?"

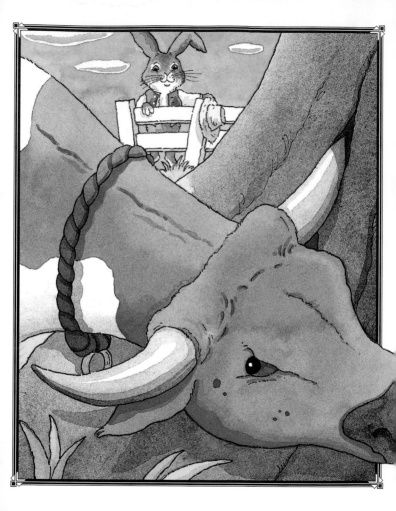

"Oh, proper poorly," says she. "I just can't pull my horn free from his tree."

"Why," said Brer Rabbit. "Can I be of assistance?"

"Oh yes," says Miss Cow. "If you stood behind me and pulled my tail hard, why, you might just pull me free."

But Brer Rabbit just smiled kinda slow and said,

"You do the pulling, Sis Cow, and I'll do your

grunting for you!" Well,
Miss Cow was so mad that
she pulled her horn from
the hole and chased Brer
Rabbit down the road as fast
as she could.

Suddenly Brer Rabbit saw a handy briar patch and in he jumped. Round the corner came Miss Cow and she skidded to a halt. Brer Rabbit stuck his head out and his eyes were as big and as round as two of Miss Meadows' best saucers.

"Hello, Sis Cow!" called Brer Rabbit in a squeaky voice. "Where are you heading in such a hurry?"

"Did you see Brer Rabbit, Brer Big-Eyes?" she asked.

"He ran past just a minute ago," said Brer Rabbit, and with that Miss Cow charged off down the road and Brer Rabbit just lay back in that briar patch and laughed till his sides ached.

Brer Fox was after him, Brer Buzzard was after him, Sis Cow was after him — but they hadn't caught him yet!